WORDY BiRDY

MEETS MR. COUGARPANTS

For Frances Gilbert—much!

—T.S.

For Sara and Sonya

—D.M.

The Library of Congress has cataloged the hardcover edition of this work as follows:
Names: Sauer, Tammi, author. | Mottram, Dave, illustrator.
Title: Wordy Birdy meets Mr. Cougarpants / by Tammi Sauer ; illustrated by Dave Mottram.
Description: First edition. | New York : Doubleday, [2019]
Summary: "When Wordy Birdy and her friends go on a camping trip, they get an unexpected visit from
Mr. Cougarpants. Can Wordy Birdy talk herself out of becoming dinner?" —Provided by publisher.
Identifiers: LCCN 2018001394 (print) | LCCN 2018008833 (ebook)
ISBN 978-1-5247-1933-3 (hc) | ISBN 978-1-5247-1931-9 (glb) | ISBN 978-1-5247-1936-4 (ebk)
Subjects: | CYAC: Camping—Fiction. | Birds—Fiction. | Puma—Fiction. | Animals—Fiction. | Conversation—Fiction.
Classification: LCC PZ7.S2502 Wok 2019 (print) | LCC PZ7.S2502 (ebook) | DDC [E]—dc23

ISBN 978-0-593-30343-6 (pbk)

MANUFACTURED IN CHINA

10 9 8 7 6 5 4 3 2 1

First Dragonfly Books Edition

WORDY BiRDY
MEETS MR. COUGARPANTS

Written by Tammi Sauer Illustrated by Dave Mottram

Dragonfly Books ⟶ New York

In case you haven't heard, this is Wordy Birdy.

I LOVE my name.
Wordy Birdy. Wordy Birdy. Wordy Birdy.
Hey! That rhymes!

Like cat
and bat
and rat

and sat and rhinoceros

and splat and—
oh, wait a minute...

Wordy Birdy is a little chatty.

Okay, fine. Wordy Birdy is super chatty. She talks all day long. Even when she shouldn't.

One day, Wordy Birdy goes camping with her friends.
Of course, she has *lots* to say.

Get comfy, readers. This might take a while.
I love this trail and I love that stream
and I love this cloud and I love that cloud
and I love my backpack and I love the view and I . . .

And I love these hills and I love this tree and I love that tree
and I love my friends and I love the moon and I love Jupiter and . . .
Do you get the picture?

Late that night, Squirrel rubs his eyes.

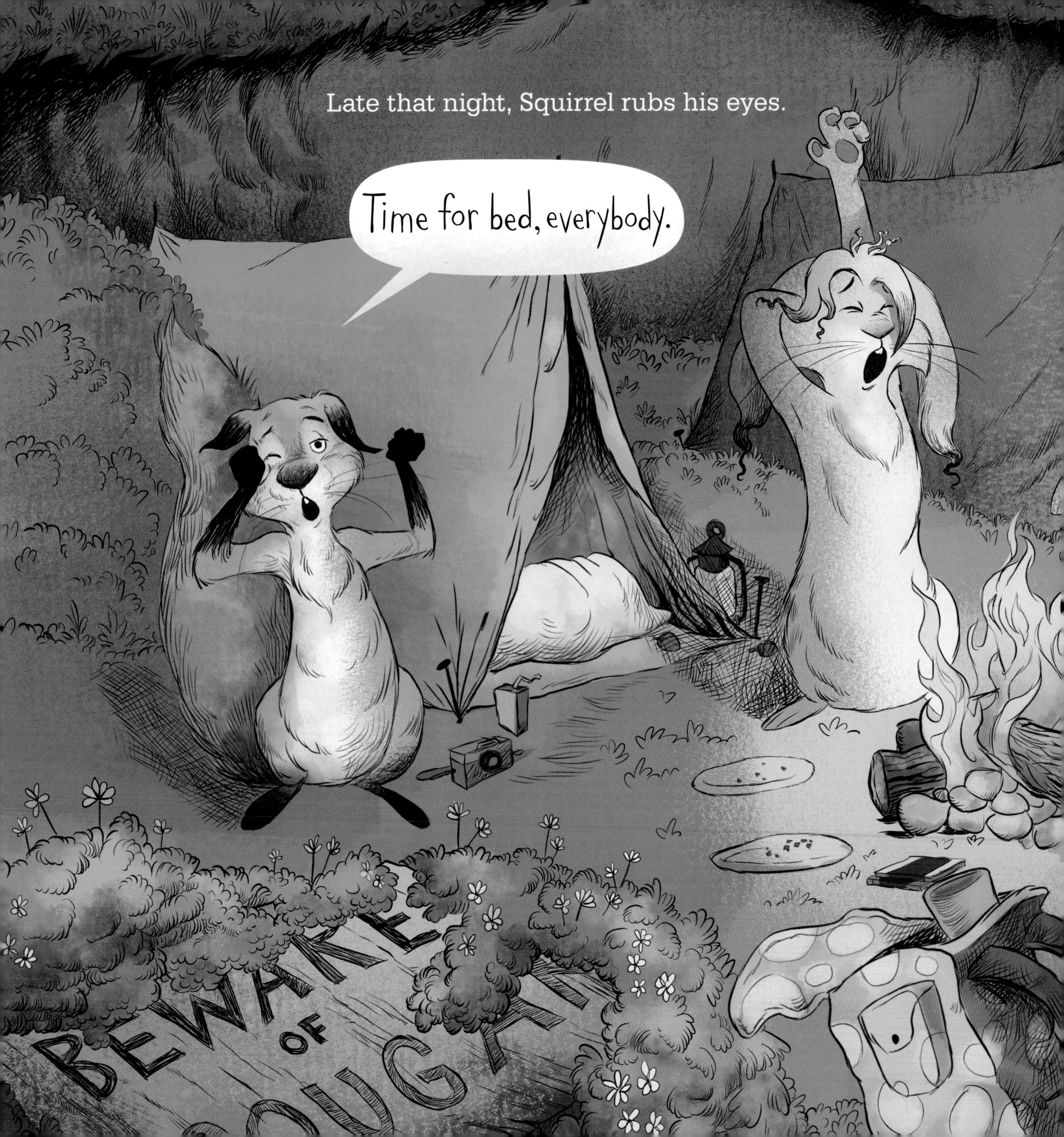

Squirrel goes to bed.
Rabbit goes to bed.
Raccoon goes to bed.
Does Wordy Birdy go to bed?

She does not.
Hey! Almost forgot! Snacks!
I brought pickles and bean burritos and more pickles
and mashed potatoes and some pickles and . . .
BAG O' BURRITOS
PICKLES

At last, Wordy Birdy finishes snacking.
Then Rabbit yawns.

Good night, everybody.

Rabbit shuts his eyes.
Raccoon shuts his eyes.
Squirrel shuts his eyes.
Does Wordy Birdy shut her eyes?

At last, Wordy Birdy finishes wishing.

I have an idea. Let's play the quiet game.

Raccoon gets quiet.
Squirrel gets quiet.
Rabbit gets quiet.
Does Wordy Birdy get quiet when a big,
hungry cougar wants to gobble them all up?

Just so you know, Mr. Cougarpants, rabbits taste terrible and raccoons taste terrible and squirrels taste really, really terrible and . . .
BAG O' BURRITOS

Did she just call me Mr. Cougarpants?
And as for me? Let's face it, I'm too adorable to eat.
Just look at this beak and these eyeballs. Even my toes are cute!
Perhaps I could interest you in a pickle and some mashed potatoes and a bean burrito and a pickle and . . .

Mr. Cougarpants can't take this one more minute.
He turns and flees into the deep, deep, *peaceful* woods.

Wow!

You saved us!

Now, THAT was a surprise ending!

Wordy Birdy is still chatty.
Sometimes she's *too* chatty.

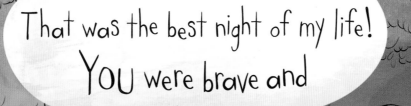

But her friends wouldn't
want her any other way.